This book belongs to:

_____

To my son Henry for his unfailing faith in his mum, and to
Malachy Doyle, without whom *Share!* would never have been written. A.S.

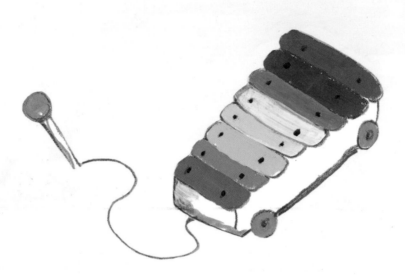

First published in Great Britain in 2010 by Andersen Press Ltd.,
20 Vauxhall Bridge Road, London SW1V 2SA.
Published in Australia by Random House Australia Pty.,
Level 3, 100 Pacific Highway, North Sydney, NSW 2060.
Text copyright © Anthea Simmons, 2010.
Illustration copyright © Georgie Birkett, 2010.
The rights of Anthea Simmons and Georgie Birkett to be identified
as the author and illustrator of this work have been asserted by them
in accordance with the Copyright, Designs and Patents Act, 1988.
All rights reserved.
Colour separated in Switzerland by Photolitho AG, Zürich.
Printed and bound in Malaysia by Tien Wah Press.

10   9   8   7   6   5   4   3

British Library Cataloguing in Publication Data available.
ISBN 978 1 84939 220 4
This book has been printed on acid-free paper

Share!

Anthea Simmons
Georgie Birkett

Andersen Press

I love my fluffy teddy,

but Baby wants him, too.

"Share," says Mummy . . .

. . . so I do.

And now my teddy's soggy and stickied up with food.

I love my book of animals,
but Baby wants it, too.

"Share," says Mummy . . .

. . . SO I do.

Now the book's all bendy
and the pages sort of glued.

I love my number puzzle, but Baby wants it, too.

"Share," says Mummy . . .

. . . SO I do.

Now the puzzle's messy and the pieces are all chewed.

I love my snugly blanket, but Baby wants it, too. **"Share,"** says Mummy . . .

. . . SO I do.

Now my blanket's yucky
and soaked right through.

My bestest treat for tea-time!
Does Baby want it, too?

"**Shall I Share?**" I ask Mummy . . .

. . . SO I do.

But Baby can't eat waffles,
he's got no teeth to chew.

I'm drinking from my cow mug. Does Baby want to, too?

"**Shall I Share?**" I ask Mummy . . .

. . . so I do.

But Baby can't do drinking,
so now he's soggy, too.

I'm painting on my easel and Baby wants to, too.

"Shall I Share?" I ask Mummy...

Now Baby's hair's got paint on
and his hands and feet are blue.

I want a bath with bubbles
and Baby wants one, too.

"Shall I Share?" I ask Mummy...
... SO I do.

Now we're clean and shiny
and warm and sleepy, too.

Baby's put in my bed
and I want to get in, too.

"Share?" smiles Baby . . .
. . . SO I do.

It's all cosy with my brother and sort of special, too.

And we're laughing, laughing, laughing, and I love him so, **I do!**

Mummy comes to hug us,
and we want to hug her, too.
"Shall we **share** our Mummy?"

So we do!

Also by Anthea Simmons and Georgie Birkett

9781849395267